W9-CAH-742

Dear Parents and Teachers,

In an easy-reader format, **My Readers** introduce classic stories to children who are learning to read. Although favorite characters and time-tested tales are the basis for **My Readers**, the books tell completely new stories and are freshly and beautifully illustrated.

My Readers are available in three levels:

1 **Level One** is for the emergent reader and features repetitive language and word clues in the illustrations.

2 **Level Two** is for more advanced readers who still need support saying and understanding some words. Stories are longer with word clues in the illustrations.

3 **Level Three** is for independent, fluent readers who enjoy working out occasional unfamiliar words. The stories are longer and divided into chapters.

Encourage children to select books based on interests, not reading levels. Read aloud with children, showing them how to use the illustrations for clues. With adult guidance and rereading, children will eventually read the desired book on their own.

Here are some ways you might want to use this book with children:

- Talk about the title and the cover illustrations. Encourage the child to use these to predict what the story is about.
- Discuss the interior illustrations and try to piece together a story based on the pictures. Does the child want to change or adjust his first prediction?
- After children reread a story, suggest they retell or act out a favorite part.

My Readers will not only help children become readers, they will serve as an introduction to some of the finest classic children's books available today.

—LAURA ROBB
Educator and Reading Consultant

For activities and reading tips, visit myreadersonline.com.

To Jacob and Hannah
—M. H.

SQUARE
FISH

An Imprint of Macmillan Children's Publishing Group

PETER PAN. Text copyright © 2012 by Susan Hill.
Illustrations copyright © 2012 by Michael Hague. All rights reserved.
Printed in China by South China Printing Company Ltd.,
Dongguan City, Guangdong Province. For information, address
Square Fish, 175 Fifth Avenue, New York, NY 10010.

Library of Congress Cataloging-in-Publication Data
Hill, Susan.
Peter Pan : lost and found / story by Susan Hill ; illustrated by Michael Hague. — 1st ed.
p. cm. — (My readers. Level 2)
Summary: Jealous of Peter Pan's new friend Wendy, who can tell stories,
Tinkerbell tries to find Peter's lost shadow.
[1. Fantasy. 2. Friendship—Fiction. 3. Lost and found possessions—
Fiction. 4. Fairies—Fiction.] I. Hague, Michael, ill. II. Barrie, J. M.
(James Matthew), 1860–1937. Peter Pan. III. Title. IV. Title: Lost and found.
PZ7.L8582Pe 2012 [E]—dc23 2011030975

ISBN 978-1-250-00452-9 (hardcover)
1 3 5 7 9 10 8 6 4 2

ISBN 978-1-250-00459-8 (paperback)
1 3 5 7 9 10 8 6 4 2

Book design by Patrick Collins/Véronique Lefèvre Sweet

Square Fish logo designed by Filomena Tuosto

First Edition: 2012

myreadersonline.com
mackids.com

This is a Level 2 book

LEXILE: 590L

Peter Pan
Lost and Found

Susan Hill • illustrated by Michael Hague
inspired by J. M. Barrie's *Peter Pan*

SQUARE
FISH

Macmillan Children's Publishing Group
New York

All children grow up—

all except Peter Pan.

When he was very young,

Peter ran away to Neverland,

where he could be a boy forever.

Peter didn't have parents,
but he did have a very dear friend,
the fairy Tinker Bell.
Tinker Bell was so small that
she could fit inside Peter's pocket,
if he'd had one.

Peter didn't mind not having parents,
but he did wish he had someone
to tell him a story,
especially at bedtime.

One night, Peter decided

to find a story.

"Come with me,"

Peter said to Tinker Bell,

and they flew out of Neverland.

They flew until they heard

a girl's sweet voice saying,

"Once upon a time."

Peter and Tink snuck in a window.

They listened to a girl named Wendy

tell a story about Tom Thumb.

"Humph," said Tinker Bell.

She spoke in fairy words,

which sounded like the tinkle of bells.

Tink wanted to be the one

to tell Peter Pan a story,

but she didn't know any.

Suddenly, Wendy saw Peter.

Peter and Tink flew away,

but not before the dog

got Peter's shadow in her teeth.

After Peter and Tink flew home,

Tinker Bell chimed loudly.

"What is it, Tink?" Peter asked.

Tink pointed at the shadow of a tree.

She pointed to the ground

behind Peter.

"But there's nothing there!"

said Peter.

Then Peter understood.

"Where in the world is my shadow?"

he cried.

"That dog must have snapped it off!"

Peter and Tink flew back

to Wendy's house.

"There you are!" said Wendy.

Peter forgot all about his shadow.

He forgot about Tinker Bell.

"What about that story
you were telling?"
Peter asked Wendy.

"It has a happy ending!" Wendy said.

Tink couldn't tell Peter a story,

but she would find Peter's shadow!

She looked in a drawer.

She started to look in pockets.

Wendy saw the open drawer

and shut it with a bang.

Tinker Bell was trapped inside!

"Does anyone hear a tinkling sound?"

asked Wendy.

Peter opened the drawer.

Tink flew out in a fury

and threw Peter's shadow

to the floor.

Then she flew away,

trailing the sound of angry bells.

"Clever Tink," Peter said.

"She found my shadow!"

Wendy took out a needle and thread.

With careful stitches,

she sewed Peter's shadow to his feet.

"Clever Wendy," Peter said.

"That didn't hurt a bit!"

Then, with a wave,

Peter flew out into the night.

"Don't go, Peter!" Wendy cried.

"Please come back!

I know lots of stories!"

Back in Neverland, Tink was still angry.

"Wendy didn't mean to shut you

in the drawer," Peter said.

"Is that what's got you all a-jingle?"

Tinker Bell shook her head.

She pointed to Peter's heart.

She pointed to her own heart.

Peter understood.

"Wendy is my new friend,"

Peter said.

"And you are my dear old friend.

There's room in my pocket for both."

Tink tugged on Peter's shirt.

"I very well know

I have no pockets," Peter said.

"By pocket, I meant heart."

Tink's laugh rang

as bright as gold bells.

"Now come along, Tink,"

said Peter Pan.

"Let's find out how the story ends."